Dear Parents:

Congratulations! Your child is taking the first steps on an exciting journey. The destination? Independent reading!

STEP INTO READING® will help your child get there. The program offers five steps to reading success. Each step includes fun stories and colorful art or photographs. In addition to original fiction and books with favorite characters, there are Step into Reading Non-Fiction Readers, Phonics Readers and Boxed Sets, Sticker Readers, and Comic Readers—a complete literacy program with something to interest every child.

Learning to Read, Step by Step!

Ready to Read   Preschool–Kindergarten
• big type and easy words • rhyme and rhythm • picture clues
For children who know the alphabet and are eager to begin reading.

Reading with Help   Preschool–Grade 1
• basic vocabulary • short sentences • simple stories
For children who recognize familiar words and sound out new words with help.

Reading on Your Own   Grades 1–3
• engaging characters • easy-to-follow plots • popular topics
For children who are ready to read on their own.

Reading Paragraphs   Grades 2–3
• challenging vocabulary • short paragraphs • exciting stories
For newly independent readers who read simple sentences with confidence.

Ready for Chapters   Grades 2–4
• chapters • longer paragraphs • full-color art
For children who want to take the plunge into chapter books but still like colorful pictures.

STEP INTO READING® is designed to give every child a successful reading experience. The grade levels are only guides; children will progress through the steps at their own speed, developing confidence in their reading.

Remember, a lifetime love of reading starts with a single step!

Step into Reading, Random House, and the Random House colophon are registered trademarks of Penguin Random House LLC.

Visit us on the Web!
StepIntoReading.com
randomhousekids.com

Educators and librarians, for a variety of teaching tools, visit us at RHTeachersLibrarians.com

ISBN 978-0-399-55906-8 (trade) — ISBN 978-0-399-55907-5 (lib. bdg.)
ISBN 978-0-399-55908-2 (ebook)

Printed in the United States of America
10 9 8 7 6

STEP INTO READING®

STEP 3

READING ON YOUR OWN

DREAMWORKS

TROLLS

PØPPY'S PARTY

by Frank Berrios

illustrated by Fabio Laguna,
Gabriella Matta, and Francesco Legramandi

Random House New York

This is Troll Village.

It is the happiest place—
with the happiest trees
and the happiest creatures.
They are called Trolls.
It is also the place
Poppy calls home!

Poppy loves
to dance and sing.
She also loves
to sing and dance.
And today she gets to do both!
She is very excited.

Poppy is going to throw
the biggest, loudest,
craziest party ever!
King Peppy can't wait!

Everyone is getting ready
for Poppy's party.
But first Poppy has to
pass out the invitations!

Poppy's friend Smidge

is super small but super strong.

She gives Poppy a super lift!

Poppy brings Biggie
an invitation.
He is a big softie.
He cries happy tears.

Poppy visits Creek.
He always gives good advice,
and everyone hangs on
his every word.
Creek is a super-cool Troll.

Poppy knows that Guy Diamond
will make her party shine.
He shakes off a cloud
of glitter whenever he dances!

Poppy drops in to see the twins,
Satin and Chenille.

Poppy's fashionable friends
will create awesome dresses
for her to wear before, during,
and after the party!

Poppy practices
her dance moves with Cooper.
No one can dance like Cooper.
That's because he is
the only Troll with four feet!

DJ Suki is creating a special
playlist for Poppy's after-party.
DJ Suki uses all sorts of
critters to make music.
She is always ready
to drop the beat!

Poppy's friend Fuzzbert
loves to tickle the Trolls.
He is also a tickler
on the dance floor!

Branch is a very different Troll.

He does not like to sing.

He does not like to dance.

He does not like to sing

or dance or hug!

Branch is the only Troll
who does not want to go
to Poppy's party.
Poppy and her friends
are shocked!

24

Poppy gives Branch
a special invitation.
She knows she can help him
find his true colors.
With a song in your heart,
you can do anything!

At the party, Smidge sends
glitter sparkles into the sky.
DJ Suki turns up the volume.
She makes it loud!

The Trolls sing and dance,
and hug and sing,
and dance and hug
at Poppy's biggest,
loudest, craziest
party ever!

Everything is rainbows
and cupcakes.
Hug Time!

31901061178713